Lastly, My Love

AF445821

Kirti Gupta

apk publishers
BY WRITERS. FOR WRITERS.
www.apkpublishers.com

Cover Designer:
Pritali Joharapurkar
pritali26@gmail.com

*"Look mom,
I finally finished something."*

Preface

My family owned a bookshop and an introvert kid who liked to escape into fantasies. As a side-hustle, they (both now published authors) also wrote for the local radio. In trying to emulate them and failing miserably for a few too many years, I gave up. At that time, in my head poetry always had to rhyme, which kept me unhappy with the end result.

Fast forward to the chaos of hitting puberty and discovery of the non-rhyming genre, I began again. This time it stuck and has been my outlet for venting and escapism.

I couldn't have gone through life without the support and encouragement from my awesome girl group- Dr. Binu E.E., Dr, N. Nazia R., Piu, Shradha, Manjula, Gitanjali, Nive, Pooja, Kanchan, Swati, Rita and many more. I am so blessed to have met you guys and I truly cherish our friendship.

Many thanks to my publisher Anagha from APK Publishing for helping with my first book in a smooth and non-daunting manner.

Finally, I would also like to thank myself for holding on when things got tough and seeking help when I needed it. Also, for giving me moments of pure joy and good enough health to bask in my experiences.

The learnings I now have, I wouldn't trade for the world.

You're doing a good job-me!

P.S. for my nephew: Bonu, if you are old enough to read this, come stay at my holiday home (assuming I have one by then). Also, you promised me a purple car. A custom Jaguar would be nice.

*This book is dedicated to
all the people in a dance-off with the devil.
You're my kind of people.*

About The Author

"Unpredictable", "robot", "scary", "really weird", "I'm pretty sure she's an alien" are some of the phrases used to describe the author.

We would like to assure the readers that these claims haven't been proven yet.

Kirti started writing at the age of 6 and like her parents, has written for local newspapers, AIR Port Blair and company newsletters. She works in IT as a Product Manager during the day and as a vampire-writer by night. She was never arrested and has a good track record in saying complex tongue twisters. We are investigating if she can shape-shift into a cat.

She once got lost in an airport, but it was Charles de Gaulle Paris, so it doesn't count. She prefers tea over coffee unless it is an authentic filter coffee from South India. She has two active blogs- https://aroundkirti.blogspot.com/ and a dream journal https://adventuresofzzz.blogspot.co.uk

She is against drugs and is currently working on a sci-fi fictional-mythology that is also a product of her dream visions. She also said something about a thriller-comedy but we think it's a fake genre.

Her life philosophy is- "Mind your own business".

Content

Shadows of Summer

Let me sleep in the shadows of summer
And let the leaves sing
Let me bathe in good tidings
Let me veto some feelings
Put a crown on my heart
Dish verses in silverware
Find a ledge by the window
And let me disappear there.

Clarity

Breathe deep, breathe hard
Take in the sounds that call you forward
You could walk by the river
Or simply be swept by the currents
As long as there is grass beneath your feet
Your dreams shall prevail
Fight for your fairytale!

A Sheep's Trail

She opened her eyes and they called her Penny
Travels & adventures, she thought, would be many
Innocence and hopes, she carried in her heart
Struggling with reality, but had a rough start

My dear, my dear, you are unique
But out of the boundaries, thou shall not peek
Thou shan't even try, lest you fail
Thou shall abide by the sheep's trail

Fainter the lines grew, with passing days
Horizon and stars, still holding her gaze
Paths became weary, mundane life grew
A hint of rebel sparked, out of the blue

My dear, my dear, you are unique
But out of the boundaries, thou shall not peek
Thou shan't even try, lest you fail
Thou shall abide by the sheep's trail

Wising up, she felt unhappy with finite choice
The meek yearnings, had finally gained voice
They cried- Our Penny is astray, is it a farce?
Why walk to the horizon, why want the stars?

We've laid out the rules, told you what to do
You've seen the trail, should've followed it too
The eccentricity, has to be confined
Don't talk of 'new', don't speak your mind.

My dear, my dear, you are unique
But out of the boundaries, thou shall not peek
Thou shan't even try, lest you fail
Thou shall abide by the sheep's trail.

Ashes

There is no fire left
In the ashes of yesterday
What was true
Isn't real anymore
It's a Schrodinger situation
When you are lost
All directions look the same
What you own is only your name
Everything else is ashes.

Glimmer

A whale of a bad time is going on
You've had less than half a luck
It is a fine night to feel lonely
It is a fine night to feel alone
Who would cherish the little things?
Who would revel in monotone?

A little rough weather never hurt anybody
A little stumble, doesn't take all
Buried in everyday pretence
Does a depraved fall.
Did you seek shelter from the dusk?
Did you need arms for comfort?
Haven't you been sleeping?
Or did you never wake up at all?

Come now when all seems to be over
Come now when all hope is lost
In the fabric of my old sweater
There is safety to be found
Come now the door is open
Come now, I'm still here
Come now, I've been waiting too
Come my darling, my dear.

Sunday Birdie

Look at the birds flying by
And cradle a hope in your heart
One day, when you grow wings
Someone will look out their window
At you.

A Few More Nights of This

Slow down, let's stop for a minute
Have our hearts talking
Are you sure about the bridge?
We don't have to keep walking
Catch us a few twinkles
Chasing after these fireflies
The plains are inviting
For some more dainty nights
I don't mind the open skies
I don't mind the empty spaces
You can light up my eyes
There's no need for fireplaces.

I like you just fine
Why wouldn't that suffice?
Isn't it nice?
Isn't it nice enough?

I see your boats by the lake
I am not ready to row just yet
Could I razzle-dazzle?
And make you forget?
Come on, it's a tender walk
Ifs, buts and could be's
The picture on the shore
That is just a tease

I am not the bravest
Or a misguided fool
I hear you say- all is fair
But isn't there a rule?

I like you just fine
Why wouldn't that suffice?
Isn't it nice?
Isn't it nice enough?

Mind Over Matter

There there, it's gonna be alright
Don't give up without a fight, just yet
There there, you've seen it all before
Can't say it won't hurt anymore, just yet

There's nothing wrong with being strong
And I'm not trying to flatter
It's mind over matter

Hold on to the last shred of belief
Don't get up and leave, just yet
Give yourself some solace
Don't walk from your happy place, just yet

There's nothing wrong with being strong
And I'm not trying to flatter
It's mind over matter

No one's by your side
But you don't need to hide, just yet
Don't give up without a fight
Don't give up without a fight, just yet.

Willing to Wander

I can't sleep
In the cacophony of silence
I can't dream
In the lifeless void
Barren lands and empty hands
Don't make for an optimistic green
So much is unknown, unseen
Lend me a hope
So that I may fantasize
Lend me a heart
So that I may cry
In a world starved of promise
Lend me a lie.

Changes

After a long silence
The sky finally bleeds chaos
All that was comfortable
And all that was known
Is swept away
In a blinding storm
We don't need to find shelter
We need to be consumed
And soaked to our bones

In discomfort, we metamorphosize
It is a small price
For the winds of change.

That Girl

She laughed with the wind
Like no one was listening
She danced with the sun
Like no one was looking
Who is that girl?
Without fear of tomorrow
Without regret or sorrow
Without truth or lies
With no past in her eyes
Where is she from?
Where is she from?

She dared to walk alone
On the broken bridges
I could see her wounds
In between the stitches
Who is that girl?
And why she can fly?
Why can she touch the purple sky?
Why is she so sure, without a doubt?
Why can't I even call her out?
Where is she from?
Where is she from?

It is just a word
But she lives it

Alone, birthing
A bohemian spirit
That girl
Seemed familiar
That girl
In the mirror.

Day of Roses

I'd like a day of roses
To be gazed upon and cherished
To move ever so lightly
Against someone's cheeks
I'd like to peek through fences
And invite only smiles
To put some colour
In the otherwise dull whiles
I'd like to tread on
The edges of a path
To have hands touch
Without malice, without wrath
I'd like to get caught
On someone's mane
To dance in dewdrops
To shower in the rain
I'd like a day of roses
A day well lived indeed
A day I don't have to follow
A day I don't have to lead

Your Guitar

The greys in our hair defy
All that we knew about being young
And now we see that some lines
In the melody of life, remain unsung

When the heart hops from one love to another
When with each un-kept promise, you lean further
Realizing wounds can be mended but not the scar
You aren't mine anymore but I'm keeping your guitar

Our lives are chemistry
Always reacting, always attached
After so many tries, you'll know
There's nothing called 'starting from scratch'

What we are left with, are pieces that are lent
Our original self, would only be- a percent
A broken song, a rainbow, a pair of jeans
A penny for my thoughts from my teens

A sliver of hope's echo coming from afar
I'm leaving you but I'm keeping your guitar.

Gazing Out the Window

We need but a window to dream
Even though what we see
May not be what we want
The sun would shift
The grass would change
And we would all breathe
A little easier
Knowing
The dreams that the night will bring
Couldn't all be bad
And we can all wear
Capes in our own worlds.

Ready Enough

There is sunshine, I suppose the morning is young
Coming by to knock down a day
Why does it feel that something has slipped?
Dreams or hopes, castles in the air?

It's not hard to point
When school bells changed, to meeting invites
When allowances turned to salaries
It added a knot in our minds

Are we ever ready enough
For the greys and wrinkles?
For the wedding bells?
Are we ever ready enough
To hear what she tells?

Anxious all the while
We forget to stop and smile
Who has time to see
Birds take wing to a distant isle?

Friends and mirrors on the wall
Don't travel in between spaces
Just as well, we figure
Lest they show our true faces

Are we ever ready enough
For the greys and wrinkles?
For the wedding bells?
Are we ever ready enough
To hear what she tells?

The Little Death

Wave after wave after wave
I miss the floating
Do we drown if we are anchored down?
Do we stay if we are adrift?
Silently the lines blur
When blue meets blue
Not all of us aim for horizons
Some of us just want the shore

Questions

What is this hanging in the air
A feeling of stagnancy
A fear of nothingness
Why the sense of despair?
Impediment to lunacy
Too scarred to confess?

Why are the feet bound
Trails chalked
And life boxed?
Where is the sound
Of the choked
And the taxed?

Why aren't we searching?
Why aren't we reaching?
Why aren't we running free?
Why aren't we asking?
Why are we masking?
Why don't we disagree?

Where is the meaning
In baking cakes
In knitting scarves?
Is it time for weaning
Past the aches
Into the wharves?

Where is the faith in chance
Affinity for gamble
Taste for venture?
Why not a second glance
At a chaotic scramble
Troubled by wencher?

Why aren't we searching?
Why aren't we reaching?
Why aren't we running free?
Why aren't we asking?
Why are we masking?
Why don't we disagree?

Ye Olde Friend

Hello my friend,
How have you been?
It's been so long
Since I have seen
That dimple, that smile
That sparkle in your eyes
That chuckle in your laugh
That quiver in your voice
Could we go someplace
And soak up the sky
Long time, no see
And life has passed us by

Let's rekindle the old
Over a pint of beer
Regale with our stories
In the manner of Shakespeare
Find us someplace
That doesn't track time
A little wooden, acoustic
Little musky and slime
Let me hold your hand
And warm my heart
Let me interrupt you
Before you start

Are you comfortable? Happy?
Like you used to be
Are you masking a tear?
For no one to see
You know you can tell me
You know I will listen
You know I won't judge you
I won't ask a reason
I wish I could say-
"I know you so well"
So much time has passed
And I've been through hell

Would you listen to me,
And see my defence?
Would you listen to me,
With a five year old's innocence?
Could I tell you
What I've gone through?
Could I tell you or
Would you misconstrue?
Would you be keen
In my sorrows and lows?
Do you know how it is
When it all blows?

I'll let that slide
Time is too short
Let's smile and laugh
You know what's what

Tell me about your wife
You kids, your work
Tell me when you were
Cut off by a jerk
We'll jiggle up some oldies
Over two shots
Discuss sneaked movies
And failed prank- plots

We'll smile and pretend
Like it's going swell
And tell each other
Really all seems well
It would be one of the many
Times we didn't let loose
As we've aged, we got
To fill bigger shoes
We'll shake hands and wave
Maybe throw in a hug
And this meeting would be
Swept under the rug
We'd promise to meet
Someday… later
But maybe not here
None of us tipped the waiter.

Wishes, Wishes

Give me the rainy windows
Give me the city cafes
Give me the sunset walks
And stay up till the dew forms
Raise a glass to the past
And drown the swirling stars
Lip to lip share a secret and
Fly away on the evening breeze
Breathe from a mountain top
Let your heart take the fall
Only thinking what you can say

The city is lit
Love isn't missing, is it?
Have you seen the sands?
Does it matter if we're holding hands?
If I could walk on water
I would save the drowning leaves
I don't need the snow
But just a glimpse
The cold is cruel
The view isn't
A touch of green
In the lap of the sun
Now, that's an idea for heaven

A castle in the woods
Sorrowful by the lake
Joy is what the village takes

Pebbles are all we get
Not stepping stones
Alas, the bridge from me to you
Is far from done.

A Day With a Muse

I'd like to write a love song
Upon your naked back
Let my heart loose and
Cut me a little slack
Little pecks here and
Little kisses there
Don't worry about the tangles
In love, all is fair
If I touch you with a flower
Would you darling, withdraw?
You can feel my heart too
I'm not a body made of straw
Pick me for your nights
Pick me for your days
Undo the things that I am
Charmer, teach me your ways.

Strange Places

I wish for strange places
To teach me a little magic
To hold my hand and take me
To the land between our dreams
I wish I could see wonder
In big things and in small
And find mystique and secrets
From the pockets of my teens
Hold my youth by the reins
Cradle hopes of venture
Strange places grant a chance
To live in a fantasy
Would I be using swords?
Would I be riding horses?
Take me to your princesses
Let a commoner curtsey

Strange places give me
A rumour of adventure
My knowns weigh me down
Give me an effing crown.

For a Forgotten Self

I see time has worn you down
I feel your nakedness and shame
Your innocence seems to be going
I know you're tired with the blame
I watch as blacks turn to greys
The lines get finer everyday
In the midst of it all, there still is
That song that makes you sway

You may not know what being happy is
But you can still cherish a smile
There is a long way to go but,
Rest with this tune a while
Catch a few breaths of relief
I promise, I won't be long
Close your eyes and think of me
At least until this song

You don't have to worry about the debts
You don't have to worry about the answers now
What you can dream in your happy place
Is only what you allow
Barefoot on the grass
Sunshine filtering through the trees
It's not that hard to find
The hope for a summer breeze

Won't you tiptoe a little
Around your childhood memories
And tell me again
The old shoe- box stories
Hey, hey now, be strong, you
It's not that difficult you see
You only have to look into a mirror
To catch a glimpse of me.

I've Been Meaning to Write

I've been meaning to write
But there's another excuse
From
My forgetful self

I've been meaning to write
And I wait
For the perfect words
To show themselves

I've been meaning to write
And I want you to know
All the feelings
I am yet to feel

I've been meaning to write
With pearls
And strings of gold
With flowers and teal

I've been meaning to write
As long as I have wanted
To fight
These wars within me

I've been meaning to write
For who else would voice
My fears, my joys
My stars, my valleys

I've been meaning to write
As soon as I unwrap my hands
As soon as I unburden my shoulders
As soon as I have
Another cup of tea

I would write.

Finding Solace

I've seen you fall so many times
Seen you bear so many crimes
On your soul, which is in pieces
Where's your Jesus?
Where's your Jesus, now?

When knots loosen to become a noose
And both your choices are to lose
Your morals stay defeated
Where's your Jesus?
Where's your Jesus, now?

I probably should be picking you up
But I am out of words to console
There ain't enough beer to drown the pain
Only the devil can save your soul

The words stand, repeated
Where's your Jesus?
Where's your Jesus, now?

Goodbye

With the sunset, the dusk is
Strangely heavy on my heart
We've walked towards the end
Now I don't know where to start
I thought when we grew up
We'd just sort of know-it-all
But even after many miseries
I, continue to fall
I'm too old to be pacified with hope
Too silly to be thinking aloud
Saviours are busy tending to the world
With remnants of grace, I bow out
Can't say if this is my lowest
Can't say if I'm all cried up
Can't say if my soul is innocent
Can't say if I'm still incorrupt
If all is decided
Is it worth the struggle?
There's fate, there's Karma
Why go through the trouble?
I'll leave you the horizons
And take to the sky
Here, take away your leash
I bid you goodbye.

A Year of Solitude

How long before we peer beyond our masks?
How long before we venture out of the caves?
Can we not rejoice in a hopeful future?
Must we only plant flowers for our graves?

The days got longer and shortened once more
The geese that had left, now flew back
With clipped wings, we stared at the sky
A year of solitude confined in our shacks

Where time is an illusion and life is a dream
These fairy tales we read, are not what they seem
Sunshine is dreary and water is reclusive
Entire existences revel in foreboding themes

Bound by dimensions, we have no visions
But a spoonful of our souls is sacrificed everyday
What good is your name, your work, your legacy?
What good is it all, if you are eroding away?

Muy Bien

Slowly you let the night slip
Into a sea of despair
All the good things are in the past now
What have we got to compare?
If this does deem fit to you
If you think it's the end
Muy bien
Let's just be friends

Issues and petty fights and
Wars and crimes are all so wrong
So many times, you've tossed me about
I don't know where I belong
If you think that we won't get along
If you think it's the end
Muy bien
Let's just be friends

Resentment was never the answer
Regret was never a choice
Your subconscious would have pleaded
If you ever heard its voice
If you think that this ain't for you
If you think it's a dead end
Muy bien
Let's just be friends

A New Year

Is it time to wake up?
Is it time to fly?
Is it time to be hopeful
And to say goodbye?
Is it time to tiptoe
Around new people and places?
Is it time to remember
And to forget a few faces?
Send a cautious hello
To wishes in the jar
See what dreams are made of
Find out who we are.
With each beating heart
Our feelings amplify
Until we grow wings
And take to the sky.

Why the Wait?

It could be a simple serene night
We could be strangers in clay
Or you could make me howl with the wind
And take my demons out to play
What is it that holds you back?
Don't you like it a little rough?
A lonely kiss at the end of the evening
When was that ever enough?
Teeth need to sink into flesh
Nails need to be bloody
Are you afraid of me, my dear?
Are you afraid of what we could be?

Honey it's all fair in love
If that is the word you choose
Unchain my wrists darling
Let all hell break loose
Would you rather pin down
Your desires with my hands?
And keep me waiting the night
In the rain, in the stands
Eyes have undressed us, no?
What else is left to witness
I'm waiting for us to resolve
Into a hot tangled mess

Praises will find their way
Near an exhausted dawn
I have little regard now
Little regard for vêtements
I am in the mood for a tease
But not an elaborate show
Why would you want to contain?
Why wouldn't you want to know?
I'm calling you right now
I'm calling you right here
Meet me beyond the compliant
Meet me beyond my demure

Let me breathe your name
Let me sleep with your smell
Let my fingers entangle in yours
Let all else go to hell.

When in Love

Let me tune up my guitar
And hope this song travels the distance
Remind you of little things
Like the river cruise for instance
I borrowed some cues
From the movies I made you watch
It's worth a start

Take it from me, it was just grand
When I step back, I understand
What I was, and what I became
It's just natural to want your name
You make me happy, could I say, I do?
Or would you be the one that flew?
I borrowed some cues
From the lover's galore
There's still so much more

Attraction played its part
But that was just the start
So many things came into play
Binding, freeing, making you stay
Love is a many stupid things, my sparrow
Fleeting allure is far too narrow
I borrowed some cues
From watching the trends
Hoping this day never ends.

One of the Walks

A wanderer's heart on streets unknown
The unsung melody of a silent storm
Hellos from people far and near
Walking off my unknown fears

C'est la vie, or is it?
Sometimes we blink and miss it
Mortals are bound by the clock
Do we know where to knock?

Tying us all, is it fate?
Do we all pass through the same gate?
Rational or not, fear still divides us
Until some hope and strength finds us

So, we keep walking the streets unknown
Having torrid affairs with the silent storm
Aching for love, a glance, a hello
Fearing for life when it all goes mellow.

Library

There is so much comfort in pages
My stories, my golden cages
And even if I've read you before
I'll be back for more

Take me through your heaven and hell
Follow the empires that rose and fell
Make me cry or make me scream
Or make no sense in Alice's dream

Give me my lovers, my friends, my foes
And teach me tongues that nobody knows
Holler names of dragons and knights
Take me dancing, take me to fights

Take my laughs and tears to hide
In between your lines I've lived and died

Everything's Fine

There are new depths in debasing
Some say it is easy
Losing a bit or losing a lot
Does it matter what we forgot?
It is a voluntary curtain
We pull over our eyes
And pretend everything's nice.
You see
Given a chance
We'd all take the blue pill.

Do Not Execute

The lies we tell ourselves
To be able to look up the sky
The fingers that are clenched
To hold our heads up high
There is lawlessness
In everything we do
But meander gracefully
Crushing wishes with our shoe
There is no sleep for us
There is no secret keeper
These chains of hopes and dreams
Only pull us deeper
Ride or die these hollow lies
Sink into the grime
Give up, give up, give it all up
Kafka till the end of time.

The Other Guy

Do I seem distant?
For I am a little lost
I could live in the moment
But at what cost?

You want me to forget
The way he makes me feel
You want me to believe
That this is real

His smell still lingers
His words still echo
For he knew all the
Right things to say

He made me laugh
When I was down
Took me for midnight strolls
All around the town

He knew how I liked
My chamomile
And you want me to believe
That is this is real?

His smell still lingers
His words still echo
For he knew all the
Right things to say

It's unfair to you
I couldn't do the secrecy
I love you but I'd
Rather be with my fantasy

He's loved me more
More than you could
And I'd swap the two
Of you, if I could

It probably sounds like
An unfair deal
I have a hard time believing
He isn't real

His smell still lingers
His words still echo
For he knew all the
Right things to say.

Forgiving the Past

Don't hang on to this moment
It will pass
Don't depend on youth
It will not stay
Don't take to heart
Your mistakes
Don't base it all
On today

In forty years or so
When you look back to this time
When the world won't make sense
When the songs won't rhyme
When you'll desperately search
Your memories to find
Something vague, something familiar
Something smooth, something unrefined

I won't be there
Hanging on the last thread
I won't be there
But just a regret

I don't want a could
I don't want a may
Let me just be
And slowly fade away.

Take One More Step

Some remember that sleepwalk
Inside our lonely hearts
We cannot see the road end
Only where it starts
Right now what you need
Is enough strength to stand
And a voice to whisper-
'Come here, take my hand.'
Even if it seems
A story and far-fetched
All lies are bad forever
Is a theory most alleged
Run away if you want
Run away if you must
Take care of your own
And in yourself you trust
No one else wanders
These roads in your mind
Then ask yourself something
To you, are you kind?

Best Wishes

I wish you winter suns
I wish you fleeting glances
I wish you circling bees
And colourful butterfly dances
I wish you shores in the eve
I wish you winds in your sails
I wish you dolphins in the distance
And chirpy beluga whales
I wish you green green grass
I wish you a soft carpet of moss
I wish you buttercups of dew
And a life with a cause
I wish you big hugs
And egos small
I wish you endless wishes
'Cause you deserve it all.

Rendezvous

One, two, three, four
Counting down before
I knock your door

Is that a smile I see?
Are you happy
To see me?

Pour me a drink
Wash away my fears
Keep me close
Until the storm clears

Stay up with me
Don't call it a night
Don't let me go
Not without a fight.

Be still my beating heart
It's only the start.

Am I ahead of myself?
I haven't dwelt
Or fairly had any help

Is that a smile I see?
Do you finally
Feel free?

Play some jazz noir
Fill the eve with wine
Let the inhibitions fade
Darling, be mine

Tell me what you need
Let me hear you say it
You've helped me in the dark
Now, let me pay it.

Love, still your beating heart
It's only the start.

Words in the Air

A world is hidden
Between my pages
Between two daily chores
Between the distance
Of breaths
I can close my eyes
And travel the seas
That life is such a tease.

I'm not sleepy these days
I don't long for a rest
A cup of tea is vacation enough
And a blade of grass is a gift
My eyes don't follow the sun anymore
Or find respite in spring
I don't think in "time"
What's mine will always be mine

I can close my eyes
And travel the seas
My dreams aim to please.

Desolation

Another day has gone by
I've dragged my wounded pride
I'm burnt and dusted
But I sure have tried

If I fancy evil someday
I'd throw up my arms.
Desolation has its charms.

Living isn't nail- biting
Nor is it exciting
It isn't a smooth glide
Just phantom fighting

What good is a word
If it is not spoken?
What good is a word
If it is broken?
What good is a word
It's only pages?
What good is a word
If it's been ages?

Let me fuel the pain
See if my heart warms
Desolation has its charms.

People

People
They chew you up
And spit you out
They strip you down
And accuse you of indecency

Tell me what is more indecent
Your naked thoughts
Or their cloaked assumptions?

Bits and Pieces

Little by little
I'm fading away
Little by little
I'm falling apart
Little by little
I don't feel okay
Little by little
You're breaking my heart

So silently the dark sets in
So vaguely minds go numb
Behind closed doors nightly
Silently souls succumb
The yearnings were killed
Then killed some more
All hopes bundled and
Thrown out the door
I've lost shoes that travelled
My buttons undone
Moments of clarity
Are zero to none
Little by little
I won't call your name
Little by little

I won't be the same
Little by little
I'm going away now
Little by little
Ciao!

Thunder

The gales are moving
As they move through ghost towns
For the first time I've truly felt
Why we associate 'howling' with winds
The ominous dread
Has scared the sun into hiding
As little cyclones of dust are spawned.

Trees beg for mercy
Giving up their produce,
Their flowers, their limbs
We peer silently from our windows
Listening to the clouds growling
Like a child being reprimanded.

"What have I done?" I ask, feigning innocence
And it thunders back,
"What have you ALL done!"

Coffee With Sugar

From coffee to a sunlit night
Have we been talking for ages?
Living a few pages
Is this how you dreamt it would be?
Can you come closer to me
So I can see your golden hues?
Lead me to a gentle smile
Feed my soul with your eyes.
I may be shy.

This boat has been rocked before.
I will not lie
I have the shields up.
But my worries dissolved in the cup.
You have been patient
And I want to walk some more
With you
Into the sunlit night.

Gifts on Valentine

Give me your lip
If not your word
Give me your heart
If not your shirt
Give me a thought
Give me a gaze
Give me a rainbow
In purple haze
Give me a care
Give me a touch
Give me your soul
I don't ask for too much.

Right Now, Right Here

How could I blame you for
Arresting me with your thoughts
How could I be eloquent
With my stomach in knots
Guilty I could see you never, my sweet
But imagine the could be's
Wouldn't that be neat?
It comes and goes
These feelings with you
How much could I gather
From stolen rendezvous?
"If only" I think and then
I miss it
I'm looking forward to an
Imaginary visit
Touch me a little but
Touch me not
Stay out of my fantasies
But give me a knock
All the hellos and hi's
Grow weary my dear
It's time I take you
Right now, right here.

Fervour

Raise your glass and smile with the swirls
Peeking around is mischief in curls
Songs of levity float about in pairs
We need dancing shoes, not a few chairs
Think of a wish and send it to the moon
This night isn't going anywhere too soon.

Lastly, My Love

I've kissed you
Before the sunshine
When happiness
And future rhyme
I've sung you
Songs of love
Way ahead of
My time
Upon my shadow
You are building
Hopes and dreams
But the last stretch of green
Is far away from here
Do you think I'll stay
When my life has gone away?

Here, take my love
And dress it
With your flowers
Of teatime
Give it a string of pearls
Or a necklace
Made of pine
I'll take your care
Like life has
Taken hope away

And when you call and ask
I'll say- it's okay
Do you think it is fruitful
To lie and say I am hopeful?

Let's not blame
Each other
For things we
Cannot change
I thought loving
Was simple
But you just
Found it strange
My eyes are weak
I cannot see
Beyond distance
And time
So, when you asked
What happened?
I just said-
It's fine
Do you think it could hurt
More than what it's worth?

Puddle

I jumped in a puddle
I hoped it would give me some joy
Or a childlike giggle
Maybe it would push
The button on my day, my week, my life
I don't know what I wanted to happen
I expected it would be something
Anything
Instead, I just stood there
On my muddy reflection
On my quivering hopes
With more dirt on my shoes.
I thought rain was cleansing
Now I feel the ground is trying to eat me up
Maybe it would be easier if I stay still
Through it all
And let it consume me.
Die bitch, Die!

Songs of Battle

This life is short
But hopes are high
Some wars must begin
The apocalypse is nigh
Into the mirror
Falls our lies
We try to fly
On broken skies
Nothing is just
But if you must
Be vary of
Unending thirsts
These singing meadows
In our dreams
Threaten to swallow
By their seams
From the future
Little hopes are bought
Against our past
These wars are fought.

Umm... Not Now

The timing is not the best.
I thought I'd said my goodbyes,
I thought I'd save my sighs.
Why are you here
With a twinkle in your tears?
Why do you want me to hope?
No, the timing is not the best.
I should be going now.
There's another city that hasn't hurt me.
In the absence of fights,
I grow dreary too.
I will see another sun.
I will see another moon.
I will have my tides,
And my typhoons.
You will have to wait,
Till my heart has healed.
You need to unburden,
All that you've concealed.
It isn't easy.
It is not supposed to be.
You will have to suffer through the trials too.
This is your test.
The timing is not the best.

About Tonight

Take your shirt off the hook
Close the door behind you
Leave the curtains apart
I won't walk you to your car
I won't kiss you goodbye
I won't tell you that I love you
I think you already know
In all my songs and in all my dreams
I think of you
I won't tell you that I love you
I won't tell you that tonight
You want someone else's smell
You want another haven
It's fine if you want a better choice
But don't give up on love
Don't give up on fairytales
Don't say anything goes
If I don't tell you that I love you
Who else would tell you that tonight?

For February 13th

Why corner them into love?
Why clip their wings?
Why take away their shoes?
Why battle with kings?
You are the storm.
You walk bare feet.
These promises of roses
Aren't yours to keep.
Pick a lane unknown.
Run towards the wild.
Sing hymns of the wind.
Be your own child.

Castles

Do you know how it is
To stay in the shadows?
To pull the reins on my sighs?
Do you know how many times
I have wrapped myself
In the sunshine of forbidden things?
The delicate laughs that you adore,
The colourful fluttering talks,
The button on my heart,
Are locked away from the world.
No one can see what I am
Only what I portray.
You could tiptoe on the comfort.
You could gaze upon this being.
Take me as I am-
Hidden and unseen
For what do I have to hold from you?
Who else would I tell?
This isn't a fairy tale.
If I wanted mercy
I would have prayed.
Just once I'd like moonlit dances,
But then once isn't enough.

Seek me when you escape from your shackles
Until then I will build our castle.

If death should take me before you come,
I want you to know-
There never was a key.
There never was a bind.
You were foolishly unkind, to your own
And the moments we never had
Were always the best.

Au Revoir

Before I find out more things about you
I don't like
Before I lose my threads of reason
I think we should stop talking
You are better in my imagination
I'd like to keep you there
I hate to see you go
But I'd hate more to hate you
Let's leave when there's still light
Let's leave when there are a few laughs
Let's leave like a nice dream leaves the bed
Let's leave like a crinkle on the forehead
This journey came with an end
Goodbye and Godspeed friend.

Things Like You

I thought these were your shadows
Where I found comfort
And an air of your words
In which I breathed
It wasn't until I was choking
And I turned to see
That you were long gone
And the clouds of my miseries
Hounded me like debt-collectors
Some poison had entered my veins
As all the pictures looked distorted
If I'd have known
Our time was finite
I would have slept
And never woken up.

One Day

Here's to wishful thinking
That life was as sweet
As a cold one
On a hot summer day
As relaxed as the falling leaves
Or as blissful
As the neighbourhood sparrow
Take a sip
And ignore reality for a bit
And drown in the calm of nothingness
Just smiles and sighs
For the older and wise
And keep the wishes frozen in cubes for tomorrow

Meeting

Can I just say
I came to hear your voice
Please do not
Hang your hopes on my choice
There is a ray
That led me to your door
How are you?
Answer me nothing more
Don't say hello
But let me sit down a bit
No, no this is
My first smoke since I quit
I know. It's me!
I am here
You were never
Able to mask a tear
No matter how much I try
I could just
Never cry
Didn't you want
To go over some things?
Talk finances maybe
Not our feelings
Didn't you have
Stuff that needs to be sorted?

My idea of a plan
Is pretty distorted
Can't remember
The last time I pretended
To be so severely
Disoriented
Maybe water
Is in over-supply
That isn't
A tear in my eye

In Betweens

What do you want me to do
With all this space?
You leave me wanting.
You leave unanswered.

I linger on hopes
And tiptoe on feelings.
Dying a thousand deaths
Every time you don't show up.

It means nothing to you
And that is the worst.
Because you let my mind
Fill the gaps.

You let my own head
Kill me over and over.

Shackles of Your Words

Take your adjectives
Why would you want to
Confine me in compliments?
Is this your derivation
Of how much you've known me?
Or are you setting my limits?
I walk fierce
I walk free
I know what you meant.
I will not resign to the present.

Learn to Love

Learning to live
Is learning to love

What else has the fragrance
Of leaves in the spring
If you find yourself lost
If your soul appears distraught

Learn to love
Even if it's just you
Even if no one else will
Even without a mention
Learn to love

Hidden under layers of facades
Are yearnings aplenty
The truth is simple and bare
Everyone wants a little care

Learn to love
Even when you're scared
Even if it's all for naught
Even in the rains
Learn to love

Sometimes it will pull you up
Sometimes it will drown it all
Hearts are tender and fragile
Then there's an inner child

Learn to love
Do it for your own soul
Spend it, lend it, give your all
Lighten and mend another heart
Learn to love

Learn to love
Even if it's just you.

A Welcome Delusion

You take another feather
From my wing
As I struggle to fly
Why is it you won't bid goodbye?
 Why must I choke my sighs?
Are these trials just my own?
Would I even know
What you really thought?
How you really felt?
This isn't a hand you've held
It is better to stay in the dark
And let my spirits fantasize
I can live with some lies.

Off on a Tangent

Is there more meaning
To the three words you said?
One of them was me
None of them was you.

Do I talk in riddles?
Do you know my patterns?
Can you find little hints
Or is this out of the blue?

You might have smarts
Or you let the mundane consume
Either way there isn't much
For me to brew.

Give me an effing clue!

Closing the Door on Feelings

I now have to erase all the songs
I wrote for you
But how can I unfeel these feelings
How can I drown my dreams
How can I stop walking towards you
You don't need me
You never did
I've lost my wits about me
This love is a crime
All my world is a lie
It is cursed
Blemished
And I am
Dearly holding on to denial
And laying down my heart
To bury it once more.

Onwards

I've left the flags on the hill
This isn't my fight anymore
You can have the crown and jewels
I'll take the winds and petals
This road isn't your road
Those gates aren't of my castles
We are meant to live different lives
There is no converging
Of wishes and sighs
I'll chase the horizons
You can gloat in your riches
I don't want the rivers of wine
Anymore than you want to drink dewdrops

Hey, I am still reasonable
I'll wave if we meet again
The night is long
Our friends are few
And you'll be somebody
That I once knew.

Butterflies

I like to stroll around in daydreams
Window-shopping among what-ifs
Flicking tiny pebbles in maybes
Searching for a door that fits the keys
There are some boxes I'd rather not open
There are some songs I'm afraid to sing
I might be unaware of my own audacity
Don't you tickle me with curiosity
Don't you throw me a bone
Don't you tempt me with tunes
Don't lure me away piper
I'm not that person, I'm not her

But stay a little longer here
I'd like to remember you
See me in my dreams my love
Or see me with your naked eyes
Take me walking on the sands
Fly with me to angel skies
Fly with me like butterflies
See me in my dreams my love
Or see me with your naked eyes.

I Am As You Are

I could live in the dewdrops
Of your thoughts
That disappear with the morning sun
I could live with you not knowing
Any whispers of my desires
I could stay with my dreams
Of you not knowing if I live or die

But how could I live without
Slight traces of you
Without any hints of your smile
Without you not nearly there, where I am

I am as you are
Delusional, albeit with different things
Without any misconceptions
Of what I'd want
I am as you are
In the moment
Here and now

Ritual

It is time to loosen the ties
And bring yourself to the alter
Maybe you'll live
Maybe you'll die
We'll know
After your sacrifice.

Fin

"It's a fine day to just be alive and have tea.
You have been brave, and life does get better from here."

~ **Kirti**